W9-BHL-210

E MAI
Maitland, Barbara.
The bookstore valentine

THE BOOKSTORE VALENTINE

by **Barbara Maitland**
pictures by **David LaRochelle**

PUFFIN BOOKS

PUFFIN BOOKS
Published by the Penguin Group
Penguin Putnam Books for Young Readers, 345 Hudson Street, New York, New York 10014, U.S.A.
Penguin Books Ltd, 80 Strand, London WC2R 0RL, England
Penguin Books Australia Ltd, Ringwood, Victoria, Australia
Penguin Books Canada Ltd, 10 Alcorn Avenue, Toronto, Ontario, Canada M4V 3B2
Penguin Books (N.Z.) Ltd, 182-190 Wairau Road, Auckland 10, New Zealand

Penguin Books Ltd, Registered Offices: Harmondsworth, Middlesex, England

First published in the United States of America by Puffin Books,
a division of Penguin Putnam Books for Young Readers, 2002
Published simultaneously by Dutton Children's Books

5 7 9 10 8 6

Text copyright © Barbara Maitland, 2002
Illustrations by David LaRochelle, copyright © Penguin Putnam Inc., 2002
All rights reserved

CIP Data is available upon request from the Library of Congress.

Puffin Books ISBN 0-14-230187-6

Puffin® and Easy-to-Read® are registered trademarks of Penguin Putnam Inc.
Printed in China

Reading Level 1.8

For Nancy—B.M.

For Mary Schullo and her students—D.L.

Chapter One

Mr. Brown loved his store.

It was called the Black Cat Bookstore.

The Black Cat Bookstore sold
only ghost books.

And it had a ghost!

Mr. Brown loved his cat, too.

Her name was Cobweb.

Cobweb was different from other cats.

She ate only cheese.

And she liked to play with mice!

Mr. Brown and Cobweb lived
above the store.
They always ate cheese
for breakfast.
And they always opened
the store together.

7

One morning Mr. Brown said,

"Valentine's Day is coming.

I will have a sale."

He put a sign in the window.

People saw the sign.

They came into the store and

crowded around Mr. Brown.

"There are only four days until

Valentine's Day," they said.

"We need to buy gifts."

"Do you have *The Haunted Honeymoon?*"

"Do you have *My Spooky Sweetheart?*"

"Can you gift wrap *My Boo-tiful Ghost?*"

"One at a time, please!" said Mr. Brown.

The store grew more and more crowded.

CRASH! Books fell on the floor.

Sometimes people dropped them.

Sometimes the ghost did.

Mr. Brown was very busy.

He could not pick them up.

SPOOKTACULAR
LOVE
STORIES

13

That night Mr. Brown was tired.

"Valentine's Day is coming," he told Cobweb.

"The store is so busy. I need help!"

He put a new sign in the window:

It said: HELP WANTED!

Then he and Cobweb went upstairs
to bed.

Chapter Two

The next morning Mr. Brown got up early.

He made some cheese snacks.

Then he and Cobweb went down

to the store.

A woman was waiting outside.

Mr. Brown let her in.

"My name is Miss Button," the woman said.

"I saw your sign. I like ghost books.

I would like the job."

LOVE AT FIRST FRIGHT!

20

"Good," said Mr. Brown.

"Welcome to the Black Cat Bookstore.

We have ghost books and a ghost."

He held out the cheese.

"Would you like some cheese?"

"Oh, I love cheese," said Miss Button.

Cobweb jumped up beside Miss Button.

"This is my cat, Cobweb," said Mr. Brown.

CRASH! A book fell off a shelf.

"And that was my ghost. It is special!"

"Wonderful!" said Miss Button.

"I like cats. I like ghosts, too!"

"You are perfect!" said Mr. Brown.

He blushed.

"For the job, I mean."

They got to work.

Mr. Brown sold books.

He smiled when he saw Miss Button.

Miss Button cut out paper hearts.

She put them up all over the store.

She smiled when she saw Mr. Brown.

Miss Button was putting up hearts

in the window when...

CRASH! A book fell beside her.

"Aha!" she said to the mice.

"So you are the ghost. How clever of you."

28

At the end of the day, Miss Button said,

"I have enjoyed my day."

"I have enjoyed my day, too,"

said Mr. Brown.

"I think they like each other,"

Cobweb told the mice.

Chapter Three

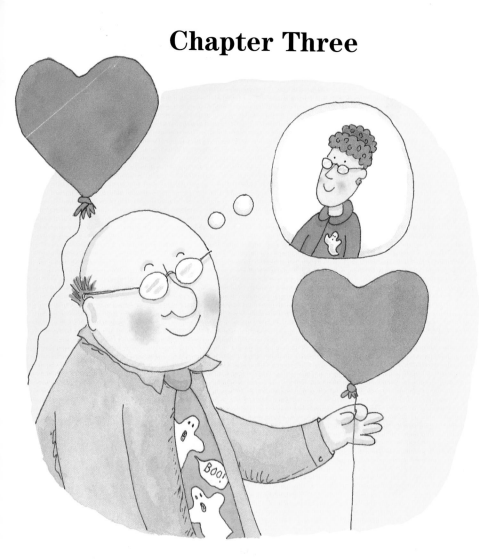

The next day, Mr. Brown put balloons

around the store.

He thought about Miss Button.

"Perfect!" he said to himself.

Miss Button sold books.

She thought about Mr. Brown.

"Wonderful!" she said to herself.

At the end of the next day, Mr. Brown said,

"Miss Button?

Tomorrow is Valentine's Day.

I was wondering if…"

"Yes?" said Miss Button.

Mr. Brown turned red.

"*Ummm . . .* nothing. I'll see you in the morning."

On Valentine's Day morning, Mr. Brown

went downstairs early.

He took a paper heart from his pocket.

He wrote on it.

MISS BUTTON, PLEASE HAVE DINNER WITH ME TONIGHT. LOVE, NORRIS BROWN

He sighed.

"What if she says no?" he asked Cobweb.

He dropped the heart in the trash can.

Mr. Brown was selling books when

Miss Button arrived.

She hung up her coat.

She took a paper heart from her bag.

She wrote on it.

Mr. Brown,
Please have dinner
with me tonight.
Love,
Emily
Button

She sighed.

"What if he says no?" she asked the mice.

She left the heart on a shelf.

Miss Button went to help Mr. Brown.

Cobweb dipped her paw in the trash can.

She fished out Mr. Brown's note.

The mice took Miss Button's note
from the shelf.

They carried it to Cobweb.

"They are too shy to send these notes,"
said the mice.

"Maybe we can help," said Cobweb.

"I have a plan."

Chapter Four

Cobweb walked over to Mr. Brown
and Miss Button.

She jumped onto a bookcase.

She dropped a note in front of Mr. Brown.

The mice dropped the other note.

It fell right in front of Miss Button.

Mr. Brown and Miss Button picked up
the notes.

They both read them out loud:

"Please have dinner with me tonight."

"Dinner would be wonderful,"

said Miss Button.

"Perfect!" said Mr. Brown.

44

At the end of the day, Miss Button and

Mr. Brown went upstairs.

Miss Button made hearts out of string cheese.

Mr. Brown made cheese pizza and

cheesecake.

Then they went back downstairs
to the bookstore.

Miss Button lit candles.

Mr. Brown put out the food.

"Can Cobweb and your ghost come to
dinner, too?" asked Miss Button.

"Ahem," said Mr. Brown. "About my ghost…"

"Don't worry, Norris," said Miss Button.

"I like mice."

"Emily, you *are* perfect!" said Mr. Brown.

They all sat together.

Mr. Brown raised his glass.

"To ghosts, Cobweb, and my

bookstore Valentine," he said.